Summer Is Summer

Phillis *and* David Gershator

illustrated by Sophie Blackall

Henry Holt and Company
New York

Henry Holt and Company, LLC
Publishers since 1866
175 Fifth Avenue
New York, New York 10010
www.henryholtchildrensbooks.com

Distributed in Canada by H. B. Fenn and Company Ltd.

Library of Congress Cataloging-in-Publication Data
Gershator, Phillis.
Summer is summer / Phillis and David Gershator ; illustrated by Sophie Blackall.—1st ed.
p. cm.
Summary: Presents a celebration of summer from a child's perspective.
ISBN-13: 978-0-8050-7444-4 / ISBN-10: 0-8050-7444-9
[1. Summer—Fiction. 2. Stories in rhyme.] I. Gershator, David. II. Blackall, Sophie, ill. III. Title.
PZ8.3.G3235Sum 2006 [E]—dc22 2005012732

First Edition—2006 / Designed by Patrick Collins
The artist used watercolor on paper to create the illustrations for this book.
Printed in China on acid-free paper. ∞

3 5 7 9 10 8 6 4 2

To Christy, for helping the roses bloom
—P. G. and D. G.

For my brother, Crispin
—S. B.

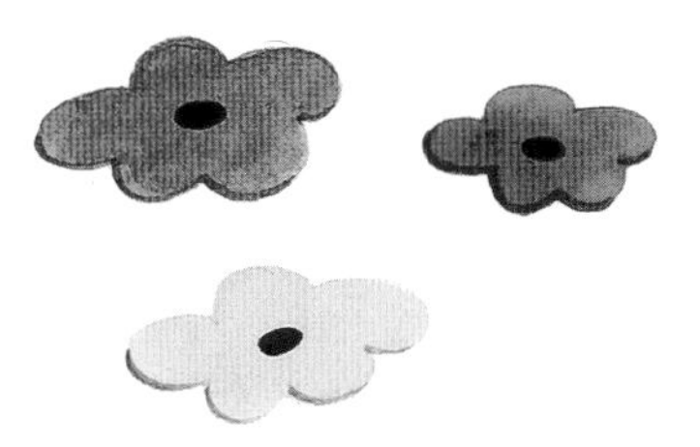

"A rose is a rose is a rose."
—Gertrude Stein (1874-1946)

A rose is a rose
And *everything* grows—
When summer is summer is summer.

A bee is a bee is a bee.
A tree is a tree is a tree.

Cool in the shade,
Pink lemonade—
Summer is summer is summer.

A hole is a hole is a hole.
A mole is a mole is a mole.

Plants and seeds,
Sneezy weeds—
Summer is summer is summer.

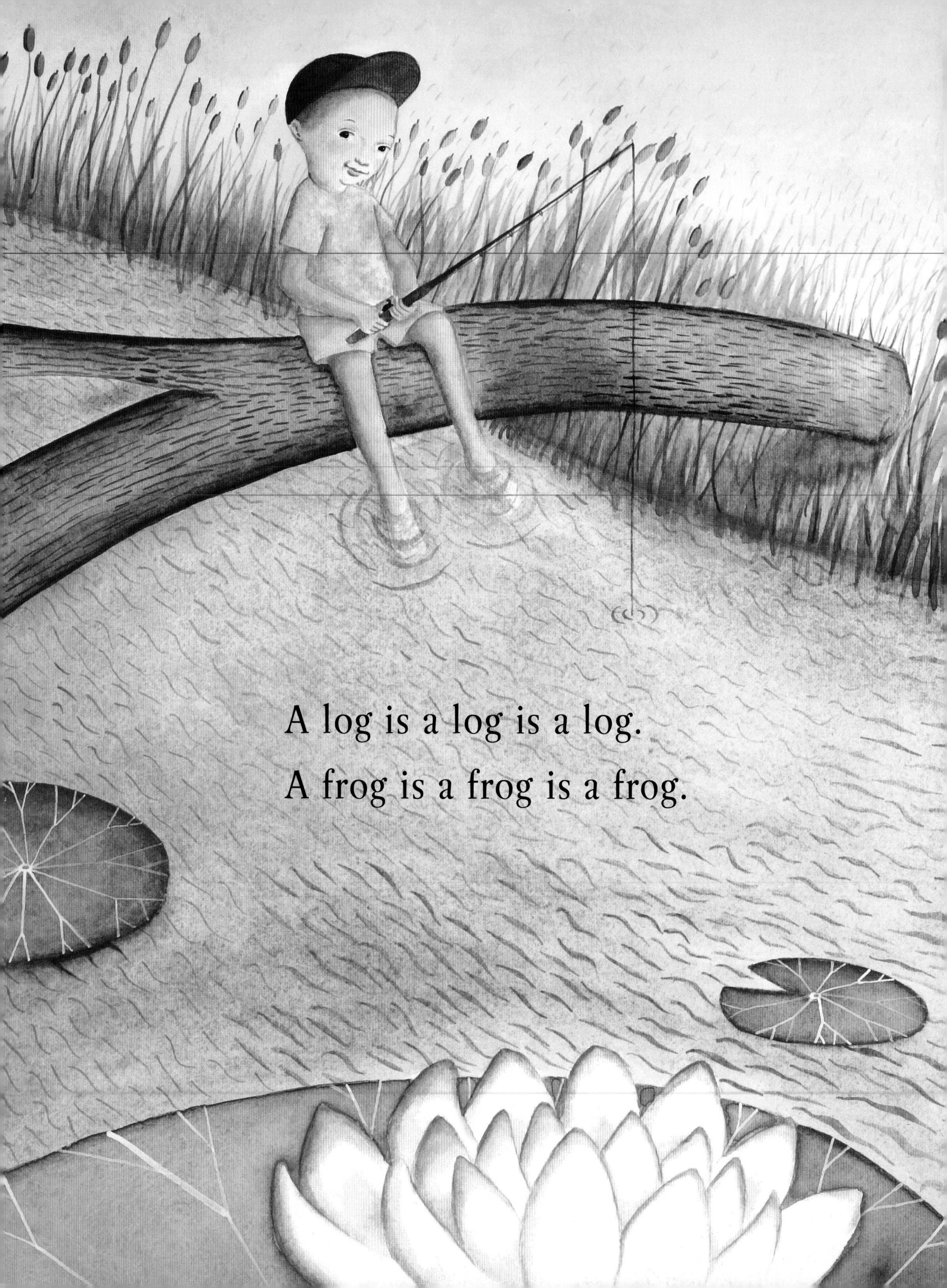

A log is a log is a log.
A frog is a frog is a frog.

Crawdad creek,
Hide-and-seek—
Summer is summer is summer.

A crowd is a crowd is a crowd.
A cloud is a cloud is a cloud.

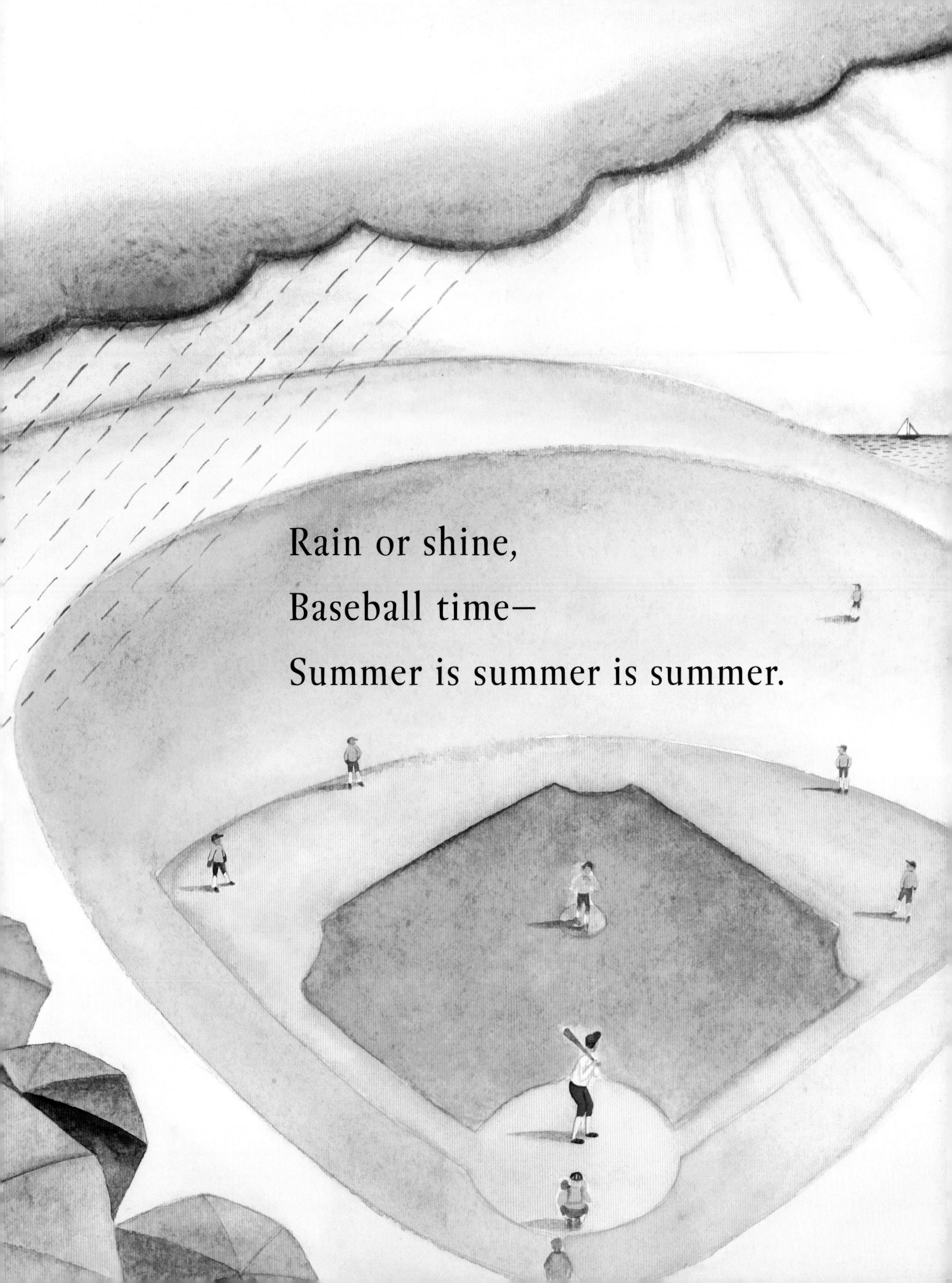

Rain or shine,
Baseball time—
Summer is summer is summer.

A sail is a sail is a sail.
A pail is a pail is a pail.

Salty air,

Sandy hair—

Summer is summer is summer.

A night is a night is a night.
A light is a light is a light.

Fireflies,
Starry skies—
Summer is summer is summer.

Watermelon,
Ice cream,
Daydream,
Night dream . . .

And that's how it goes
When a rose is a rose
And summer is summer is summer.